DA VINCI
vs THE FURNITURE OVERLORD

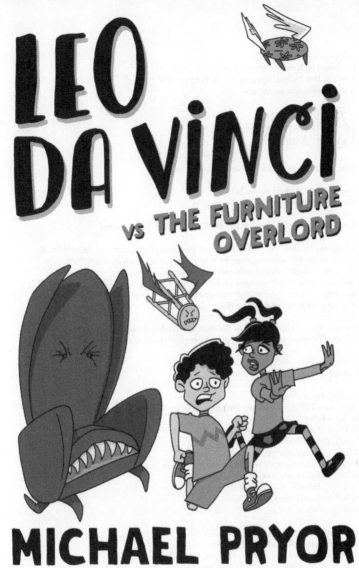

LEO DA VINCI VS THE FURNITURE OVERLORD

MICHAEL PRYOR

ILLUSTRATED BY JULES FABER

RANDOM HOUSE AUSTRALIA

A Random House book
Published by Random House Australia Pty Ltd
Level 3, 100 Pacific Highway, North Sydney NSW 2060
www.randomhouse.com.au

Penguin
Random House
Australia

First published by Random House Australia in 2016

Random House Books is part of the Penguin Random House group of companies
whose addresses can be found at global.penguinrandomhouse.com.

National Library of Australia
Cataloguing-in-Publication Entry

Author: Pryor, Michael
Title: Leo da Vinci versus the Furniture Overlord / Michael Pryor; illustrated
by Jules Faber
ISBN: 978 0 85798 839 3 (pbk)
Series: Pryor, Michael. Leo da Vinci; 2
Target audience: For primary school age
Subjects: Leonardo da Vinci, 1452–1519 – Fiction.
        Adventure stories.
        Friendship – Juvenile fiction.
Other authors/contributors: Faber, Jules
Dewey number: A823.3

Cover and internal illustrations by Jules Faber
Cover design by Rachel Lawston, Lawston Design
Internal design by Midland Typesetters, Australia
Printed in Australia by Griffin Press, an accredited ISO AS/NZS 14001:2004
Environmental Management System printer

Random House Australia uses papers that are natural, renewable and recyclable
products and made from wood grown in sustainable forests. The logging and
manufacturing processes are expected to conform to the environmental regulations
of the country of origin.

To Jane O'Brien, Richard deBoer,
Ros Drummond, Louise Counsel and Trish Calder,
with many, many thanks.

CHAPTER 1

Ten-year-old Leonardo da Vinci slipped the goldfish back into the freshly cleaned fish tank.

'All done,' he called to his mum. He wiped his hands on his shorts. 'I'll be in the shed.'

'What are you and your friends up to, Leonardo?' his mum called from the kitchen.

'We'll be monitoring supervillain activity and keeping an eye on an undersea monster off the coast of Chile.'

'That's nice, dear. Will you be saving the world again?'

'I don't think so,' Leo said. 'Not today.'

'Well, you never know,' his mother replied. 'Don't forget to take a piece of fruit with you.'

Leo grabbed a pear from the fruit bowl, then sprinted across the backyard and into the shed. 'Status report!' he barked.

The shed was the headquarters of Leo's top-secret world-saving organisation, Fixit International Inc. It was also his workshop, his laboratory and his art studio. It was possibly the most cluttered space in the entire universe.

Piles of stuff balanced on heaps of stuff that were teetering on giant mounds of stuff. Other stuff hung from the rafters while different stuff was tacked to the walls. Some stuff was on shelves, some in barrels and still more was in jars marked 'STUFF'.

Isaac the wood-burning robot and Ragnar the pig stood in the middle of the room arguing.

Ragnar turned to Leo. 'Status? Well, I've got a sore trotter. I stood on a drawing-pin that *someone* left lying around. And Isaac's right knee needs a good polish.'

'Argh, not *your* status, Ragnar!' Leo exclaimed. 'I need a worldwide update!'

The stubby chimney on Isaac's back let off a puff of smoke. 'You sound irritated,' the robot said. 'Is something troubling you?'

Leonardo da Vinci, genius inventor and guardian against evil, scowled and rubbed his forehead. 'Fixit International Inc. hasn't saved the world for nearly a month. It's making me nervous.'

Ragnar and Isaac looked at one another.

'We should tell him the news,' Isaac said.

Ragnar's eyes widened. '*Both* bits of news?'

'I think so,' the robot replied. 'You know how he gets when he hasn't saved the world for a while.'

Leo gritted his teeth. 'It's not a good news/bad news start to the day, is it?'

Isaac shook his head and then quickly grabbed it as it nearly fell off his neck. 'I'm afraid it's a bad news/bad news start to the day.'

CHAPTER 2

Leo dragged a stool out from under a bench that was buried beneath a mountain of sketches. Lately, Leo had been practising hands. Hands were tricky to draw, and he liked trying different approaches. He had drawn hands clenched, hands pointing, hands flat, hands praying, but he was never quite sure if he'd nailed it.

He sat on the stool and crossed his arms. 'Tell me. I can take it.'

Isaac finished tightening the screws on his neck and put down the screwdriver. 'We have received intelligence that suggests Wild Wilbur is planning something.'

Leo smashed his fist into his palm. Wild Wilbur was his sixth deadliest enemy. Leo had suspected he was up to something, mostly because Wild Wilbur was always up to something. Wild Wilbur wasn't terribly good at being a supervillain but he was a very determined one. He wasn't at all happy with being number six on Fixit International Inc.'s List of Most Dangerous Supervillains. He desperately wanted to make the top five.

'What is it?' Leo asked. 'Has he teamed up with awful alien invaders? Has he invented a way to turn earthworms into unstoppable killing machines?'

Ragnar snorted. 'He's borrowing books from the library.'

'Clever.' Leo rubbed his chin. 'No one would suspect that borrowing library books was the first step in an evil plan.' He frowned. 'It is the first step in his evil plan, isn't it?'

'We think so,' Isaac said. 'Especially since one of the books was called *How To Make Explosive Devices That Look Just Like Ordinary Food*.'

Leo looked at the robot in surprise. 'They have books like that at Vinci Library?'

'They do indeed, young sir,' Isaac said. 'They're very popular. Irresponsible but popular.'

'And where did you get this information?' Leo asked.

Isaac pointed at the shimmering, tinkling SlinkyScope, the massive communications board that filled nearly one whole wall of the shed. Leonardo had made it out of dozens of slinkys. It was the only communications screen he knew of that could walk down stairs. 'We have arrangements with many useful organisations in Vinci,' Isaac said. 'They send us updates about any suspicious activity.'

'So you're in regular touch with the library?' Leo said.

'Whenever they notice suspicious borrowing patterns,' Isaac replied. He picked at a bit of rust on his elbow.

Ragnar made a rude noise. This was easy,

really, since his snout was extra-good at making rude noises. 'Isaac talks to the library *all* the time. He's sweet on the automated check-out kiosk.'

Isaac shrugged. 'We're just good friends.'

Leo was intrigued by this whole friendship business. After Mina came along and showed him that having a friend was a positive thing, Leo had been determined to be a tip-top friend. He had plans to create a list about what made a tip-top friend. Then he could be one. But getting his day organised came first.

'What was the second bit of bad news?' he asked.

Ragnar scratched his head with a trotter. 'Now, what was it again? Oh, that's right. Another shadowy organisation of super-evil is trying to take over the world.'

Leo shot to his feet. 'I knew it! International Fixit Inc. to the rescue!'

'Well, it was just a matter of time,' Ragnar said. 'Wait long enough around here and a supervillain is bound to turn up. I guess we're lucky that way.'

The door to the shed flew open. A figure stood in the doorway, outlined against the bright light of the sunny day.

For a split second, it looked as if a supervillain had dropped by for a visit. Then Mina, Leo's friend and second-in-command, stepped forward.

'Did you know there's a pie on the doorstep?' she asked.

CHAPTER 3

Isaac took the pie and carefully placed it in a glass trough full of water. 'It's safe,' he announced after a minute or two. 'And, might I say, it's a terrible beginner's effort.'

Everyone crowded around the trough. The pie was sitting on the bottom and it was a soggy brown mess.

'Is it edible?' Ragnar asked.

The others looked at him.

'What?' Ragnar huffed. 'It's pie!'

'Actually, I think it's made of cardboard,' said Isaac.

The pig leaned forward. 'Still . . .'

'Wild Wilbur is quick off the mark,' Leo said. 'We really must do something about him.'

'Oh, come on,' Ragnar said. 'He's sort of good to have around. Makes us feel needed, you know?'

Isaac reached into the trough and tore the cardboard apart to reveal three bright-red cylinders connected by wires. 'Instead of dynamite, he's used candles and has written "TNT" on them,' the robot observed.

Leo shook his fist in the air. 'We *must* do

something about Wild Wilbur! Mina, add him to the To-do List.'

'We're starting lists all of a sudden?' Mina looked around the room. 'Okay, where's the whiteboard?'

Leo stopped his fist-shaking. 'I replaced it with the Whiter-Than-Whiteboard.'

Mina frowned. 'Whiter-Than-Whiteboard?'

'I used the same principle as washing powder,' Leo explained. 'Why put up with a dull, ordinary whiteboard when we can have an even whiter whiteboard?'

'It sounds like an improvement,' Mina conceded. 'So where's it hiding?'

'It's under that curtain next to the SlinkyScope. It's been drying but should be ready now.'

Mina bounded over and whipped aside the curtain and all darkness vanished. The headquarters of International Fixit Inc. was filled with the most blinding light. The few shadows that were left looked at each other and decided to head for the hills. Mina reeled back and covered her eyes. 'Yowza! Leo, you should have warned me!'

Ragnar squealed and dived under a pile of sketches. Isaac clanked and slapped his hands over his overloaded eyes with a sound like a giant gong.

Leo held up a hand to shade his eyes. 'I did say it was whiter than white.'

Mina fumbled around in her pocket and pulled out a pair of sunglasses. 'That's a bit better,' she said, after putting them on, 'but it still looks like this place is in the middle of the desert in summer at midday.'

Leo stumbled to a bench near the door. He'd left some welding goggles there after his prototype of a revolutionary one-person submarine had failed. It didn't really matter, because he'd had an idea of turning the mini sub into a new kind of ski jump. Sure, it'd take a bit of work but that was half the fun.

Leo found the goggles and snapped them on. He could now look directly at the Whiter-Than-Whiteboard without fear of his eyeballs bursting into flames.

'Shut it off!' Ragnar wailed, from somewhere beneath the pile of sketches. 'Save this stuff for our enemies!'

'What setting is it on now?' Leo asked Mina.

'Eye-blaster,' she replied.

'Better dial it back a bit,' Leo said.

Mina turned the dial halfway back and the light reflecting from the Whiter-Than-Whiteboard dimmed slightly. 'Why would you even have a setting like "eye-blaster", anyway?' she said, shaking her head. 'That's crazy stuff, Leo.'

Leonardo da Vinci, clear-sighted fighter

against injustice, pulled off his goggles. He winced as his hair got caught in the strap. 'Sometimes it helps to be a little crazy in this inventing business.'

CHAPTER
4

Ragnar snorted and poked his head out of the pile of sketches. 'A *little* crazy? Leo, you are full-on crazy and well on your way to gaga crazy.'

'No time for that now,' Leo said. 'Mina, first things first – the To-do List.'

'So do I put "Make To-do List" at the top?' she asked.

'I think we can skip that, since we're actually doing it right now,' Leo replied.

Mina nodded. 'Good point. You know, Leo, I think this is a great idea. I mean, it's cool that we save the world and everything, but it probably helps if we're organised while we're doing it.'

'My thoughts exactly, Second-in-Command Mina.'

Mina took up a permanent marker. 'Wild Wilbur is item number one, right?'

'Not exactly,' Leo said. 'Isaac, tell us about the new dangerous threat to the entire world.'

'There are hints that we could be facing a new menace,' the robot began.

'Isaac has been keeping an eye on the Wikipedia "World Threats" page,' Ragnar explained.

'It's very useful,' Isaac said, 'and it's updated quite regularly.'

'Okay.' Mina stood on the tips of her toes. 'So I'll put "Unknown but dangerous menace" at the top of the list?'

'Yes, and Wild Wilbur can go to the bottom for now,' Leo said.

Ragnar eyed the trough. 'Are you sure? That pie could have been dangerous. If I'd eaten it, I mean.'

'I think we'll risk it,' Leo said. 'But let's be alert for any other strange edible objects.'

Ragnar brightened at this. 'I volunteer to dispose of any non-strange edible objects.'

'And put "Order more Kitties HiLo

merchandise" near the top,' Leo added. 'People can't get enough of them.'

Kitties HiLo was the invention that earned Leo the most money – buckets and buckets of it. They were the two cutest cat characters in the world, the bestest of friends – one big, one small, with extra-smiley faces. As soon as Leo had drawn them, he knew they were winners. Now they were on merchandise everywhere.

The SlinkyScope chimed. Leo was proud of that chime. He'd investigated the sounds of bells and had come up with a combination that was specifically designed to be both surprising and charming.

'I've had the SlinkyScope scanning for any major disturbances,' Isaac said. 'Something's just come up.'

The screen wobbled and then a face appeared. It was a young boy who looked to be around Leo's age. He had straight black hair and wore a wooden crown. Only his chest and shoulders were showing, but Leo could see that he was wearing a fur cloak over a horribly bulky costume.

'And there's our supervillain,' Leo declared.

'How do you know?' Mina asked.

Leo gestured to the screen. 'Watch.'

'I am the Furniture Overlord,' the super-villain announced. 'Soon the whole world will bow down before me!'

'See?' Leo said. 'It's all in the costume.'

CHAPTER 5

'The Furniture Overlord.' Mina tapped her chin thoughtfully. 'Sounds confused.'

'Maybe he's multi-tasking,' Ragnar piped up. 'Conquering the world but selling lounge suites in his spare time.'

'Shhh,' Leo hissed. 'He's still talking.'

'No need to bow all at once, of course,' the Furniture Overlord continued. 'It would be silly if everyone in the whole world bowed down at the same time. Bus drivers, for example, shouldn't bow. It would make driving a bus very difficult.' He paused. 'But that's not important. What *is* important is that I will soon conquer the world with my killer furniture army!'

The Furniture Overlord sat back, looking satisfied. He glanced down at his notes and surprise flickered across his face.

'Oh, I mean the world has already been infiltrated by my top-secret squads of killer furniture. They are currently in disguise in your homes, your offices and your public spaces. They are ready and waiting for my command. When you least expect it, they will strike. Will it be your umbrella stand? Or will it be your footstool?'

'No!' Ragnar cried out. 'Not the foot-stools! Anything but them!' The pig paused and saw the looks that Leo, Mina and Isaac were giving him. 'Sorry. I got carried away.'

The Furniture Overlord pointed at the camera. 'I have chosen the City of Vinci as the first to feel my might. Tremble, all of you, at the power of the Furniture Overlord!'

The image cut out and the SlinkyScope wobbled back to normal.

'Well, as crazy world-dominating plans go, this one is definitely unique,' Mina said. 'Turning furniture against us? That's creative.'

'It might be creative,' Leo said, 'but we

have to stop it. Supervillains can't be allowed to have their evil ways.'

Mina scratched her head. 'How come all the supervillains I've met seem to be about our age, Leo?'

Leo turned to Isaac. 'Does the My Little Brainy have any statistics on this?'

My Little Brainy was one of Leo's most ambitious experiments. He'd always wanted to create a living, organic computer. So one day he took a jar of peanut butter, the mould off some old cheese, a pair of tired, unwashed socks and a dozen eggs that were *way* past their use-by date and bathed it all in some leftover chicken soup his mum had made. Now wrinkly and throbbing and about the size of a watermelon, the My Little Brainy lived in a transparent box next to the SlinkyScope.

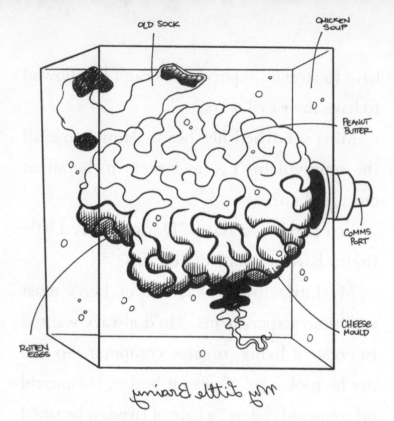

OLD SOCK

CHICKEN SOUP

PEANUT BUTTER

COMMS PORT

CHEESE MOULD

ROTTEN EGGS

My little Brainy

Only Isaac could communicate with it, which was odd considering that he had a metal brain. Leo just took it as a sign of how strange and wonderful friendship was.

Even though he'd thought a lot about it, the concept of friendship continued to puzzle

Leo. Mina said she was his friend, but he still wasn't sure how friendship worked. And Leo really liked knowing how things worked.

'Certainly,' Isaac said. He stuck a finger in one of the sockets of the transparent cube. My Little Brainy gave off a bubble or two. 'Apparently ninety per cent of all supervillains we know about are between the ages of eight and twelve. Only one per cent are over the age of twenty-three.'

'And what's the reason for this?' Mina pressed. 'Better education? Hormones in chicken?'

'I'd say it's just that kids are the best,' Leo said. He held out his fist and Mina gave it a bump-twist-bump. Leo nodded. He'd learnt that a special gesture like that was part of being friends. He made a mental note to add it to the What Makes A Good Friend List.

The SlinkyScope chimed again.

'Oh no!' Isaac threw his hands up in the air. When they came down again, he had to get Mina to screw them back on. 'It's a major alert!'

'I hope so,' Ragnar said. 'I wouldn't want to see you panic like this if it was only a minor alert.'

Isaac peered at the screen. 'We have a code-red disturbance!'

'What's the location?' Leo demanded.

'The Vinci Homemaker Centre,' Isaac replied.

'Sounds like the work of the Furniture Overlord,' Leo declared. 'Quick, to Basement Level 5!'

CHAPTER
6

The Small Lift only took seconds to whisk
them to Basement Level 5. On the way, they
went past Basement Level 1 (sculpture and
art materials), Basement Level 2 (inventions
in progress), Basement Level 3 (the Mighty
Fabricator) and Basement Level 4 (Kitties
HiLo design studio and merchandise).

Basement Level 5 was the home of some of Leo's transport inventions. He sprinted past the HiRoller. (Instead of wheels, it had hundreds of thousands of marbles underneath. It didn't work very well.) He raced past the Dread Sled. (A scary heavy-duty icemaker on top of a black wagon on runners. Not much good in the summer.) He zoomed past the Livewire Flier. (A hedge trimmer mooshed with a high-pressure water cleaner. It needed more work.)

Finally, Leo stopped in front of his latest high-speed vehicle. It was black and silver, long and sleek, with some really cool flames he'd spent ages painting on. The flames spelled out the name: Thunder Raid Lightning Thing.

'Everyone in!' he ordered.

Mina shook her head. 'You've hit a rough patch with your naming, Leo.'

'You don't like it?' he asked.

Mina shook her head again.

'Let's put that on the list, then,' Leo said. 'Make better names for inventions.'

'Will do,' Mina said. 'Now, stand aside. It's my turn to pilot, remember?'

Leo pointed at the entrance hatch. 'It's your turn from now on, you mean.'

The International Fixit Inc. headquarters had been a little dull lately. With no evil enemies on the horizon, Leo had used the time to teach Mina all about piloting the range of weird vehicles he'd invented. It had taken his second-in-command about a microsecond to get the hang of it. Mina was a natural, and it wasn't long before Leo realised that she was much better at it than he was.

Since Mina had joined Fixit International Inc., Leo had been constantly surprised by her. Not just by her jokes, either — which he had been studying hard so that one day he could crack one or two — but by just about everything. She was a good fixer too, always on the lookout for things to repair. And, well, she was just all-round excellent. It was good to have her on the team and good to have her as a friend.

Mina hesitated at the hatch. 'That's not a problem for you? Me piloting your inventions?'

'The day I stand in the way of the best person for the job,' Leo said, straightening, 'I want you to kick me.'

'Ooh, can I be in charge of that?' Ragnar asked as he clambered into the craft. 'I think a "Kicking People" department could become a vital part of International Fixit Inc.'

'Put it on the list,' Leo said.

Mina ran a safety check once everyone had fastened their seatbelts. Then she hit the 'Start' button and gave the thumbs up when the engines rumbled to life. She trundled the Thunder Raid Lightning Thing down the aisle, past the dozens of air, sea and land vehicles Leo had made. Some had been successful. Some hadn't. Some were dazzling. Some looked like they were made from leftover pasta.

As they arrived at the end of the aisle, the huge doors of the Really Big Lift slid back

and Mina carefully manoeuvred the Thunder
Raid Lightning Thing into it.

'Hold on!' Mina called.

CHAPTER 7

Leo looked at Ragnar on the other side of the narrow craft. Ragnar was strapped in and wearing his favourite Kitties HiLo helmet. Leo glanced over at Isaac. The robot's eyes were closed and his chimney was nervously puffing away. The smoke was sucked through the special vent over his head that Leo had installed.

The Really Big Lift shot upwards, and Leo's stomach fell to somewhere near his ankles. The Really Big Lift burst through the hidden hatch at the bottom of the garden and kept rising until it was metres in the air. His stomach gamely struggled upwards too. When the Really Big Lift stopped suddenly, his stomach overshot. It bounced off the back of his teeth before it fell back to where it belonged. It sat there grumbling for a second or two before Mina engaged the Fastest Drive. (She was right – Leo's naming was getting worse.)

The Thunder Raid Lightning Thing blasted through the sky and headed for the Vinci Homemaker Centre. Leo monitored

the craft, making sure that everything was in good working order. He had green lights everywhere except for the popcorn maker. This worried him. He liked popcorn.

Leo's dad had taken him to the Vinci Homemaker Centre too many times. It was a whole bunch of big shops that sold electrical appliances, carpets and lots and lots of furniture. One of the biggest shops sold furniture you had to put together yourself. A few hours of helping his dad with that sort of stuff drove Leo crazy. Leo liked assembling his own creations, but this furniture was *never* right. The instructions were so bad and the pieces never fitted together properly. It was nightmare material.

The Thunder Raid Lightning Thing split the air over the Homemaker Centre. Isaac was glued to the screen that Leo had made out of a Kitties HiLo piano tuner. Isaac was glued there because he was paying close attention, but also because he'd been trying to glue back a loose fingertip and it had all gone horribly wrong.

'I say, it's a riot down there,' he reported.

'Bring us around again, Mina!' Leo shouted, holding on tight to the Emergency Handhold Strut he'd installed for moments like this.

Leo's stomach complained as Mina turned the Thunder Raid Lightning Thing in a wicked curve. He peered out the window. Hundreds of people were running about screaming. Cars were jammed together as they tried to get out of the carpark. Even the big balloon men with flailing arms looked nervous.

'What's going on?' Mina yelled above the roar of the Double SuperGood Engines.

'I can't make it out,' Leo said. 'Bring us down in the corner of the carpark and we'll get a better view.'

Mina nodded and, with the barest of bumps, settled the Thunder Raid Lightning Thing onto the asphalt.

CHAPTER 8

Ragnar held up a trotter. 'I'll stay here . . . to protect the Thunder Raid Lightning Thing.'

'Good thinking, Ragnar,' Leo said. 'Those who stay behind probably have the most dangerous job of all.'

The pig blinked. 'You know, I think the good old Thunder Raid Lightning Thing is pretty safe. I mean, we'll lock it up before we leave.'

'Good to have you with us, Ragnar,' Leo said. He rubbed his hands together. 'Now it's weapons time.'

'Oh yeah!' Ragnar wriggled with excitement. 'Weapons time is the happiest time! Well, apart from cake time, that is.'

Leo opened a locker. 'Here,' he said, throwing a weapon to Mina. 'That's the Peanut Butter Launcher. Sticky and deadly.'

She caught it and grinned. 'Lock and load.'

'Isaac, the MultiTowel Whip for you.' Leo was proud of the MultiTowel Whip. He got the idea one day when he snapped his beach towel and it gave a loud *crack*. The MultiTowel

Whip used a dozen super-strong lengths of fabric. When snapped by a robot arm, it REALLY stung.

'Ah, delightful,' the robot said. He whirled it over his head and gave it a good crack.

It made Leo's ears ring. 'Keep that for the enemy,' he advised before turning to Ragnar. 'Now, I can strap a snout-controlled Lamington Accelerator onto your back. Are you up to it?'

'Let me at 'em,' the pig said. 'When they get a face full of chocolate and coconut, they'll be sorry they ever tangled with me.'

'Right.' Leo peered into the locker and pulled out a long, black double-barrelled number – the Tornado Gun. He'd lashed half-a-dozen egg beaters in series and powered the whole lot with an inverted tesseract he'd had lying around. It shot out a whirlwind nearly fifty metres long, so it wasn't much good indoors but it was handy in, say, a carpark or a hundred hectares of desert.

Leo hit the button that opened the hatch. When the doors slid back, a man ran past, crying out, 'The cupboards are coming! The cupboards are *COMING*!'

'Cupboards?' Isaac shifted from foot to foot. 'We'll need to be careful, then.'

'Ha!' Leo pushed forward. 'I'm not scared of cupboards.'

'The customers are,' Isaac pointed out. 'They've all run away.'

Silence had fallen over the Vinci Home-maker Centre. The only sound was the flapping arms of the giant balloon men.

Leo's heart pounded. His palms sweated.

Clutching the Tornado Gun, he eased out of the hatch. He stood there, staring, as he waited for the others to join him.

'Listen,' he whispered. 'I want every member of International Fixit Inc. who thinks we're up against dozens of hostile pieces of furniture to put his or her hand up. Ragnar, I'll count a trotter as a hand in your case.'

Two hands and a trotter shot up.

Leo added his. 'Good. For a second I thought I was dreaming.'

Facing them, and filling the carpark, was a furniture army. They'd already smashed shopfronts and crumpled cars. They jostled and lumbered towards International Fixit Inc., making nasty woody noises. Chair legs bumped against bedheads, which knocked against kitchen stools, which slammed against

coffee tables. Chubby couches jostled with easychairs. Standard lamps bounced up and down like eager ostriches. Two coat racks tangled with each other. One fell over and was accidentally trampled by the other.

Leo swallowed. This was *definitely* the work of the Furniture Overlord!

CHAPTER
9

Leo had never seen furniture moving without the help of big, burly men and a truck. 'This doesn't have to get violent,' he said to the others. 'Let's try talking first.'

'Talking to furniture?' Ragnar said. 'You want to sit down and chat with a chesterfield? Natter with a nightstand? Debate with a divan?'

'Something like that,' Leo said, giving Ragnar a hard stare, 'but without so much snark.'

'It's worth a try, Leo,' Mina said. She had her Peanut Butter Launcher clamped under one arm as she tied her hair back with a ribbon. 'But I don't like the way that chest of

drawers is looking at us. I think we've interrupted its rampaging.'

Mina pointed at a tall four-drawer model
with chrome handles. Leo saw what she meant.
It was leaning towards them aggressively.

'Look out!' Ragnar yelped. 'They're coming
for us!'

The ground began to shake.

As one, the horde of furniture rumbled towards the Thunder Raid Lightning Thing. A floral sofa bed led the charge, opening and closing like a giant bear trap. Wardrobes snapped their doors. Desks and tables galloped on all fours. Chairs clattered and hopped.

'Eat cake, woodentops!' Ragnar snarled. He nudged his snout controls. A barrage of fist-sized lamingtons hurtled at the advancing army.

One of the lamingtons hit a full-length mirror. It slid down the glass surface, leaving a sticky trail, but the mirror continued to shuffle forward. The rest of the furniture took heavy hits too, but they still kept on coming.

Ragnar squealed and backed away. 'Uh,

guys, I think I left something back in the Thunder Raid Lightning Thing . . .'

'Easy, Ragnar,' Leo said, patting his Tornado Gun. 'We'll be all right.'

'That's great,' Mina said, 'because I don't think my Peanut Butter Launcher will be much good here.'

'And my MultiTowel Whip seems better suited to more human foes,' Isaac said.

Leo made a mental note to check all weapons before setting out in future, to make sure they were right for the task ahead. In fact, that was another item for the To-do List.

'Don't worry. Just stand back – everything's under control.' Leo took two steps forward. He lifted the Tornado Gun to his shoulder. 'Cover your ears!' he warned before pulling the trigger.

A whirling funnel of air sprang from the Tornado Gun. Immediately, the front row was caught up. Bookshelves jerked up into the air. Bunk beds were flung aside. Card tables were spun around so suddenly that their legs folded and they became airborne.

'Good shooting,' Ragnar crowed. 'Take that, you plywood bullies!'

CHAPTER 10

Splinters and sawdust rained down from the sky. Leo would have liked to say that the furniture looked scared, but instead of showing fear, the next row of furniture surged forward. A band of sturdy wine racks crunched right over the remains of their former comrades.

Leo shook his head. It was clear that they were dealing with some heartless brutes here. Of course, they were also dealing with headless, armless and bodiless brutes, but that's the way with furniture.

'Hit 'em again!' Ragnar howled.

'I support that,' Isaac said. 'We do seem to be surrounded, after all.'

Leo glanced over his shoulder. It was true. A troop of fierce-looking rocking chairs had snuck up behind them. They'd joined with a bunch of computer desks and a hefty recliner on the other side of the Thunder Raid Lightning Thing. They were fast closing in.

Mina whirled and fronted them. She looked grim. She held up a large roll of duct tape and shook it menacingly at the advancing rocking chairs. 'This is high-quality, top-grade, industrial-strength duct tape – don't make me use it!' she warned.

A grating noise came from somewhere behind them. Leo swung around. The front rank of wine racks was now only metres away. Leo could see the morning light glinting off the chrome.

Leo pulled the trigger. The wine racks were bowled over, twisting and turning round and round. It was as if they were in an invisible washing machine, except that what came out at the end wasn't clean clothes, it was a massive pile of shredded wood and bent metal.

For a second Leo was distracted by an idea for a washing machine where the clothes stayed still while being blasted by rotating high-powered water pumps.

The pile of debris exploded as a pair of billiard tables burst through like wild rhinos. The billiard tables shook splinters off their green baize tops and reared up on their hind legs, getting ready to charge. Behind them was a row of tough-looking chests of drawers. They were flanked by an array of smaller furniture – magazine racks, footstools and ottomans. Is it 'ottomans' or 'ottomen'? Leo wondered for a stupid amount of time. The smaller furniture hopped about like terriers keen to get hold of something tasty.

Leo backed away. 'We might need to conduct a strategic retreat,' he yelled over his shoulder. 'We'll head back to headquarters and return with proper equipment.'

But there was no answer.

Keeping one eye on the advancing hordes of hostile furniture, he looked behind him. What he saw nearly made him drop his Tornado Gun.

CHAPTER 11

Mina ran towards the nasty rocking chairs, brandishing the roll of duct tape in one hand. She bobbed and weaved as they tried to hem her in. She leapt over rockers, kicked aside doorstoppers and jumped from seat to seat.

Leo stared, gobsmacked. He knew that

Mina was brave and clever, but this was a side of her he'd never seen.

Meanwhile, Ragnar had shrugged off the Lamington Accelerator and had the other end of the tape in his mouth. He was a porky blur as he galloped underneath the rocking chairs, going so fast that their attempts to squash him were hopeless. He went left and right, zig-zagging wildly.

Leo took a step towards them. Surely he could help.

'Stay back!' Mina cried out. 'Don't get in the way!' She bounced, flipped and leapt over the angry rocking chairs and reached the door of the Thunder Raid Lightning Thing.

Ragnar and Leo bounded across to join them. Ragnar spat out his end of the tape. 'Ew! That stuff tastes awful!'

Mina slashed the tape. She caught the loose end and threw it at what was now a mess of struggling fake antique furniture – a solid mass that was blocking the rest of the attackers.

It was a sight that, for a second, Leo really wanted to sketch. He thought it would make an impressive mural. He'd call it *The Defeat of the Rocking Chairs*.

'I didn't know you could bounce around like that,' Leo said to Mina. 'You were amazing.'

Smiling, Mina shook her head. 'You mean you never noticed me going off to gymnastics training? Or talking about gymnastics? Or practising backflips and somersaults? Sometimes, Leo, I wonder about you.'

Leo nodded. He wondered about himself sometimes.

'They're still coming!' Ragnar yelped.

Leo swung around to see another wave of furniture tumbling out of the Vinci Home-maker Centre. Umbrella stands. Trundle beds. Kitchen stools. Swarms and swarms of them! There was only one thing for it.

'Everyone, behind me,' he growled. 'I'm turning the Tornado Gun up to Setting 11.'

'To what?' Mina said.

'He has this top-secret eleventh setting on all of his weapons,' Ragnar explained while using his snout to push Mina to safety. 'For emergencies.'

'Emergencies like this,' Leo said. 'Cover your ears.'

He fumbled for the secret switch on the

Tornado Gun. He clicked it to Setting 11.
Then, slowly, he pulled the trigger.

'Wait!' Ragnar squealed. 'Where's Isaac?'

But it was too late — Leo had already
pressed the button.

CHAPTER 12

Leo had to hold tight as the Tornado Gun bucked and shook. For the few seconds it was blasting away, it took every bit of his strength to hang on. Finally, the Tornado Gun began to sputter. It coughed. It burped. Then it stopped.

Leo wiped his face. Not a single piece of furniture had been left untouched. The Tornado Gun had smashed them all to pieces. It had also demolished a row of shops, about a dozen rubbish skips, quite a few cars and a fence or two.

Leo sighed. Sometimes that was the price you paid when battling supervillains and their deadly minions. Of course, the mayor and the people of Vinci were always quick to hand Fixit International Inc. a bill for damages. He imagined the next one was going to be a biggie.

Leo was nearly knocked over by a piggy snout.

'Isaac! Where's Isaac?' Ragnar said. He was trotting in anxious circles, scanning the debris. 'Has anyone seen him?'

'I haven't,' Mina admitted. Her hair had come out of the ribbon she'd used to tie it back. 'Have you, Leo?'

Leo shook his head. He scanned the heaps and piles of broken furniture. 'The last time I saw him he was wrestling a pair of coffee tables.'

'That means he got caught up in your tornado.' Ragnar burst into tears. 'Oh no! Isaac, my best bot buddy, gone! All gone!'

Mina gasped and pointed to something behind them. 'Look!'

Ragnar and Leo turned to see a figure crawling from the rubble. 'Isaac!' Leo cried.

'Isaac?' Ragnar shook the tears from his eyes. 'You guys had better not tell him I got all broken up when I thought he'd been twisted to pieces, okay?'

'Your secret is safe with us,' Leo said solemnly.

Slowly, the ancient wood-burning robot stood up. He used one hand to adjust his knees, then he straightened his neck. He kicked aside some throw cushions. 'I have a prisoner!' he declared.

Over his shoulder was a lumpy red velvet beanbag.

CHAPTER 13

Back at the headquarters of Fixit International Inc., Leo quickly made a cage for the beanbag. Isaac stuffed the prisoner into it. Mina placed a bowl of water inside, just in case it got thirsty.

'But it doesn't have a mouth,' Leo pointed out. 'How can it drink?'

Mina shrugged. 'Maybe it can soak up water through its skin, like a toad.'

'Toads can do that?' Leo was amazed.

'I read it somewhere,' Mina said. 'Anyway, we don't need to be cruel just because it's our prisoner.'

'I've got something on the SlinkyScope,' Ragnar called out. 'I think it's Count Carpet.'

Leo dusted his hands. 'You mean the Furniture Overlord?'

'Whatever,' Ragnar said. 'He's ranting again.'

Ragnar nosed the SlinkyScope controls. The image cleared to show the Furniture Overlord in his awful supervillain costume, complete with crown.

'By now you have seen what I can do,' he boomed. 'Understand that this was a tiny demonstration of my AWESOME power. If you do not surrender, I will unleash my bloodthirsty furniture commandos!' He threw his head back and laughed.

Leo had to admit it wasn't bad for a super-villain laugh. The Furniture Overlord must have practised a lot to get it that good.

'You have three days! If I am not declared

Ruler of the World by then, your worst nightmares will come true!' The Furniture Overlord frowned. 'Maybe not the one about only being able to run really slowly from the thing that's chasing you, or the one where you're falling. Not those. Doesn't matter.' He laughed again, but it wasn't as good as the last time.

The image faded.

'Thanks to the SlinkyScope, I managed to intercept that message,' Ragnar said. 'No one else saw it.'

'So no one knows about the deadline?' Leo said. He smashed his fist into his palm. 'Good. All we have to do is find this Furniture Overlord and defeat him and then all will be well.'

'Three days?' Mina said. 'Easy.'

Leo dialled the Whiter-Than-Whiteboard right down to 'Soothing' so it was a calm, milky colour. 'If we're to defeat this evil evildoer,' Leo said, 'we first need to know where he is.'

'We've been unable to find any trace of his whereabouts,' Isaac admitted. 'Even My Little Brainy has no idea. It's sulking now.'

Leo glanced at the transparent tank. The blob in the bottom looked the same as usual. He guessed you had to be a close friend to tell the difference between a happy blob and a sulking one.

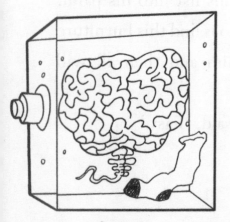

SULKING

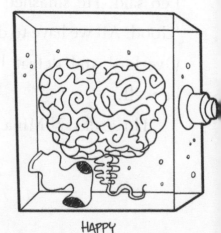

HAPPY

'It's going to be tough,' Ragnar said. 'There's nothing in the "Contact us" section of his website and nothing on social media. He's clever.'

Mina frowned. 'He has a website? A social media presence?'

'Sure,' Ragnar said. 'He might be a loony supervillain with dreams of conquering the world, but he knows the importance of a good public face. He has a logo and everything.'

He pointed at the SlinkyScope. The logo for the Furniture Overlord was a blocky set of tables and chairs. Leo grimaced. He could have designed a better logo with one hand tied behind his back. With *both* hands tied behind his back, even.

'So this would suggest that he has a secret hide-out, then,' Leo said. 'A lair, perhaps.'

'Maybe a citadel of evil?' Mina suggested. 'With really nice interior decor?'

Ragnar sniggered. 'You've got that look on your face, Leo. That "I've got a plan" look.'

'Is *that* what it is?' Mina said. 'I thought he had a headache.'

'There's no time for headaches.' Leo shook his fist. 'We have an enemy to defeat.'

'To *find* and then defeat,' Mina pointed out.

'And that's where our prisoner comes in,' Leo said.

As one, they all looked at the cage. The red velvet beanbag was hunched up in the corner. The bowl of water lay beside it, untouched.

'I don't think it'll reveal where the Furniture Overlord's lair is,' Mina said. 'I'm not sure it can talk, for a start.'

'That's not what I was thinking,' Leo said. 'I was thinking that this could be a Homing Beanbag.'

'Homing Beanbag?' Isaac repeated. 'I've never heard of such a thing.'

'How can you tell?' Mina asked.

Leo waved a hand in the air. 'It's in the stitching.'

'Oh.' Mina looked at the beanbag and frowned. 'I think it's listening.'

'Quick,' Leo said. 'Huddle.'

They formed a circle and put their heads together.

'I get it,' Ragnar whispered. 'You want to set it free and then follow it all the way back to the Furniture Overlord's lair of evil solitude, right?'

Leo rubbed his hands together. 'All I need

is to implant it with a tracking device, run a few tests and tomorrow we'll be set.'

'Sounds good.' Mina was already heading for the door. 'And don't forget that English homework, Leo.'

Leo looked up. 'What English homework?'

'We have to write a story from the point of view of a fridge,' Mina replied.

A joke popped into Leo's head. He thought about it, turned it around, looked at it and decided it was safe to go ahead. 'I have to pretend to be a fridge?' he said. 'Cool.'

Mina grinned. 'Keep it up, Leo. You'll get the hang of this humour business one day.'

CHAPTER
14

The next morning Leo's father was at the stove cooking breakfast. Leo quickly grabbed a plate. His dad made great food. Leo liked eating in his restaurant whenever he had a chance.

His dad looked over his shoulder. 'Poached

eggs, roasted tomatoes, bacon and mush-rooms coming right up. You make the toast.'

Leo cut two slices from the loaf that was waiting for him on the bench. While he measured them against each other, to make sure they'd toast evenly, he started thinking about painting another portrait of his dad – maybe with his saxophone, to show another side of him. That'd be good.

'Toast ready?' his dad asked.

'Not quite.' Leo popped the bread in the toaster.

'How's the world-saving going, Leo?' His dad pushed the mushrooms around in the pan.

'We're up against some very organised supervillains at the moment,' Leo said. 'And some disorganised ones, too,' he added, remembering Wild Wilbur's latest efforts.

'Sounds as though they're keeping you busy.'

The toast popped up. Leo buttered the slices, slid them onto his plate and handed it to his dad, who loaded it up with tasty goodness.

Leo's mouth watered. 'Thanks.'

His dad studied him for a moment before giving him the plate. 'You know, Leo, it's good to see Mina around here so much.'

'Mina?' Leo nodded. 'She's a very useful member of Fixit International Inc.'

'I think she's more than that. I think she's a good friend.'

Leo thought for a moment. 'What would you say is the most important part of being a friend?'

His dad wiped his hands on his apron. 'Trust,' he said.

'Trust?'

'Friends trust friends when times are tough.'

Leo took his plate and headed for the shed. 'Then I think Mina's a good friend too.'

CHAPTER 15

Leo entered the shed to find Isaac, Ragnar and Mina already there. They were crowded around the SlinkyScope, discussing all the possible locations of the Furniture Overlord's evil citadel of doom.

'Any luck?' Leo asked, wading through the sea of sketches covering the shed floor.

'Nothing certain,' Isaac reported. 'Too many possibilities.'

'That's right,' Ragnar said. 'Too many mountain tops. Too many lonely islands. Too many polar wastes. There's so much super-villain real estate out there. We should really look into –'

He was cut short by a knock at the door.

'I'll get it.' Mina danced over before Leo could advise her to be careful. She opened the door and stood aside as a four-rotor miniature helicopter drifted in.

'That's a drone,' Leo said. 'Everyone stay back.'

'It's a drone that's carrying a fruit basket,' Mina added. 'I wonder who sent it.'

The drone hovered above the nearest bench. It settled the big basket spilling over

with grapes, bananas, apples and pears right next to Leo's half-built giant crossbow. Then it spun around and disappeared through the open door.

Isaac tapped his metal forehead. 'Did anyone actually *order* a fruit basket?'

Mina looked at Leo. 'Wild Wilbur?'

Leo nodded. 'Steady, everyone. That fruit could be deadly.'

'I'm steady as anything,' Ragnar said from where he'd retreated to – the top of a cabinet at the back of the shed.

Leo crept up to the basket, grabbing a pair of pliers along the way. He just had to get close enough to cut the red wire, then they'd all be safe. Why it was always the red wire, he had no idea. In fact, he'd been thinking about building a bomb using only red wires. That'd fool them.

As he drew close, Leo saw a note tucked in between two oranges. He held his breath and plucked it out. As he did, a *click* sounded from inside the basket.

Leo's whole life flashed before his eyes. It was so interesting that he watched it again. He was wondering if there was an extended version with some behind-the-scenes stuff when something shot up in the middle of the basket.

A sparkler. It sputtered to life, fizzing as bright sparks flitted and darted into the air. Leo waited for his thundering heart to calm a little before reading the note.

The universe started with a Big Bang — and
you're going to end with one!
Yours sincerely,
Wild Wilbur
PS I'm just getting started with this explosion
business. I hope you understand.

Leo screwed up the note and threw it into the corner. It landed on top of a huge pile of notes from other supervillains. Supervillains loved keeping in touch.

'Right,' he said, turning to Mina. '"Get Wild Wilbur" is moving up a place on the To-do List.'

Snorting, gobbling noises made Leo jump. He turned to find Ragnar snout-deep in what remained of the fruit basket.

Ragnar's mouth was full of apple, but he

still managed to grin. 'Say what you like about Wild Wilbur. He mightn't be much good at explosives, but he sure knows good fruit when he sees it.'

CHAPTER 16

Leo opened the door to the cage. 'Come on, boy. You can go now. You're free.'

He and Isaac had dragged the cage outside, but the beanbag refused to budge.

'Maybe it likes it here,' Mina said. 'Maybe we're too kind.'

Ragnar snorted. 'By giving it a bowl of water it didn't drink?'

'Mina's right,' Leo said. 'It's become attached to us.'

The beanbag squirmed a little. Was that a squirm of agreement?

'Uh-huh,' Ragnar said. 'So I guess we should hurt its feelings if we want it to go home.'

'Exactly,' Leo said.

'Er, I was only joking,' Ragnar said. 'I mean, how do you hurt a beanbag's feelings?'

'It's not something I like to do often,' Leo said. 'Sorry, Mina, but we have a world to save.'

She nodded, her smile disappearing. 'I understand.'

'I'll open the gate,' Isaac said, and he clanked across the yard.

Leo stood over the beanbag. 'Hey, beanbag, I've seen better stitching on a sack of potatoes.'

'Ouch,' Ragnar muttered. 'You've gone straight for the throat, haven't you?'

Mina nudged him. 'Shh. Let Leo get on with it.'

Ragnar grumbled, but settled.

'You call that velvet?' Leo continued. 'You're more like sandpaper than velvet.'

The beanbag shivered.

Leo hated being so unkind, but he went on. 'No one would sit on you, you know. You look about as comfortable as a rock. Two rocks. Lots and lots of rocks.'

That did it. Slowly, the beanbag wriggled out of the cage like a big caterpillar. It hesitated before creeping across the backyard to the side gate. Leo felt bad but he knew he had to be strong. Just before it reached the gate, the beanbag bent around, as if it were looking back at them. Then it wriggled through and was on its way.

Isaac closed the gate. 'I've never seen a sadder-looking beanbag,' he said.

Leo sighed. 'I know. It was nasty, but we had to do it.'

He wondered if there could have been another way. Is saving the world really worth the price of being cruel to a beanbag? Leo blinked. What was he thinking? Of course it was!

'Now,' he said, 'we just need to track that beanbag and we'll find the Furniture Overlord. It should be a piece of cake.'

'Mmm, cake,' Ragnar said. 'Has anyone got any? I haven't had enough cake lately.'

'Is it even possible for you to have enough cake?' Mina asked.

Ragnar thought about it. 'No, I don't think so. Why don't we get some and we'll see?'

'No time for cake,' Leo said firmly. 'It's beanbag-tracking time.'

He slapped his Usefulness Belt. It was a recent invention. It was covered with pouches, containers, snap hooks and loops so he could keep stuff handy and his hands free. It was also washable and could be turned into a very narrow but serviceable snow-board in an emergency. He'd packed it full of the sorts of things they'd need to battle the Furniture Overlord and his army, including one secret surprise.

He unsnapped a small box from one of the loops. 'Behold the tracking device!'

Isaac, Ragnar and Mina gathered around.

'Okay,' Mina said. 'So I'm used to this by now. I can see it looks like a Kitties HiLo lunch box with two lights stuck on top, but I know it'll really be a super-scientific quantum-level gizmo.'

'That's right.' Leo paused. 'I call it the Tracker Box. And I'm working on the name,' he said before Mina could sigh, roll her eyes or laugh out loud. 'If the green light stays lit, we're on the right track. If the red one lights up, then we're going the wrong way.'

Ragnar raised a trotter. 'What if both of them are on at the same time? And, while we're on the topic, what if they're both off at the same time?'

Leo rubbed his forehead. 'Then something's gone wrong and I'll give it to Mina to fix.'

Mina grinned and slapped her own Usefulness Belt. 'Not a problem. I've got everything I need here.'

'Have you got cake?' Ragnar said, frowning. 'Because if you don't have cake, you're missing something important.'

'Yes, yes, we'll make sure that our supplies include plenty of cake,' Leo said. 'Now, I have the perfect vehicle to follow a Homing Beanbag. To Basement Level 5!'

CHAPTER 17

Most of International Fixit Inc.'s missions needed hypersonic transport to outfox the supervillains. The Thunder Raid Lightning Thing. The Strikebird. The GoFasterThanThe-BadGuys Craft. There wasn't much call for a slow-moving, stable vehicle, which meant that Leo hadn't had a chance to use the Drift-a-long — and he'd been dying to.

The Drift-a-long was way down at the back of Basement Level 5. It took up a lot of room. The top storey of the Drift-a-long was the lift compartment. The bottom was the command module. The command module also had the engines attached to the outside.

When they reached it, Leo walked around it, looking up at the bottom of the command module. 'Looks like we're going to have to use the Really, Really Big Lift for this one,' he said.

Leo had made the Drift-a-long out of a super-long caravan (the command module) and four of the biggest jumping castles he could find (the lift compartment). He'd packed

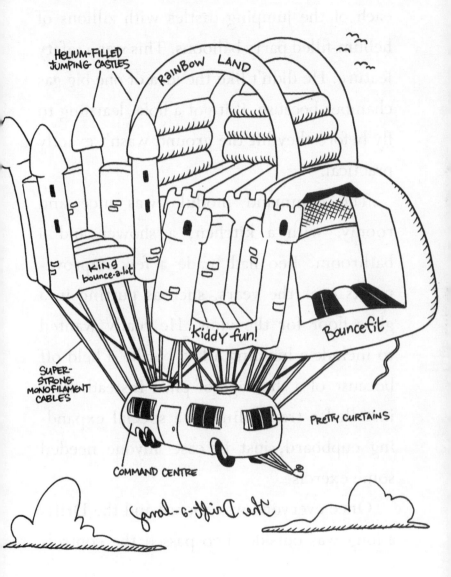

each of the jumping castles with zillions of helium-filled party balloons. This was a safety feature. He didn't like the idea of one big gas chamber because, if it got a hole, learning to fly before they hit the ground wasn't exactly practical.

The command module was nice and roomy, with a kitchen, a shower and a bathroom. Leo had made a few improvements over the years, such as putting in a glass floor for the view. He really wanted to include a bowling alley, but he'd held off because of a shortage of pins. Instead, he'd installed a trampoline in a special expanding cupboard, just in case anyone needed some exercise.

Once everyone was aboard and the Drift-a-long was outside, Leo passed the controls to Mina. 'I'm sure you can handle piloting this one.'

'Sure thing,' Mina said, studying the controls. Behind her, Isaac and Ragnar were arguing about where to put their stuff. 'Up. Down. Right. Left. Easy! What's the top speed of this monster?'

'Faster than a beanbag,' Leo replied. 'Though you could probably run faster than the Drift-a-long.'

'What?'

Leo shrugged. 'If we go any faster, we'll wobble all over the place. That's why I called it the Drift-a-long. I designed it for easygoing holidays and low-speed stargazing.'

'It's one of your better names, then,' Mina said, turning back to the controls. 'Okay, which way?'

Leo examined the Tracker Box. He shuffled around in a full circle, then pointed north-east. 'That way.'

'That way it is,' Mina said, turning the wheel. 'Off we go!'

Isaac and Ragnar came over to join them. 'Ragnar has suggested that it's lunchtime,' announced the robot.

'Good idea,' Leo said. 'I made sure that the Drift-a-long is well stocked. What about putting something together?'

'I'm onto it!' The robot clapped his hands. One of his fingers fell off, but he caught it and screwed it back on again. He glanced at Ragnar. 'I'm sure we can find some cake in there too.'

Ragnar tapped the side of his snout with a trotter. 'If there's cake, I'll sniff it out.'

They headed to the kitchen, happily dis-
agreeing over which was the best way to
slice up a cake — straight across or in neat
wedges.

CHAPTER 18

Leo pointed through the big front window of the command module. 'I can see it! There!'

The red beanbag was galumphing down the road towards the edge of town. A dachshund was staring at it and shaking its head.

'How long have we got before the

deadline?' Mina asked as she used the giant wooden wheel to steer the Drift-a-long. Leo had left the Tracker Box on the control panel, just in case Mina lost sight of the fleeing furniture.

Leo peered at a dial on the control panel. He'd taken it from a Kitties HiLo Junior Fun Alarm Clock. On the face was, of course, KittyHi and KittyLo. The hands were whiskers. It actually made Leo dizzy as he watched the hands move around. 'We have about two and a half days left.'

'Do you think the beanbag will reach the Furniture Overlord's lair by then?'

'I hope so,' Leo said grimly. 'It's the only lead we've got.'

He was worried, though. He peered at the beanbag through a pair of binoculars. It was determined but it was also slow. He frowned and looked again. Was it actually being over-taken by a snail? It couldn't be.

A few minutes later the beanbag came to rest at a shady spot under a tree. It slumped against the trunk.

Leo stared. He adjusted his binoculars, then stared again.

'You won't believe this,' he said to Mina.

'I don't know about that,' Mina replied. She was holding the Drift-a-long steady, circling over the beanbag's position. 'With everything I've seen since joining Fixit International Inc., I've become very good at believing strange stuff.'

'The beanbag just mugged a motorcyclist and stole her bike.'

Mina nodded. 'I believe it. Which way?'

'Straight ahead. Faster.'

'Got it.'

The Drift-a-long sped up. It started wobbling.

Leo made a mental note. From now on, every vehicle he invented was going to have extra handholds all over the place.

The wobbling turned into shaking.

CHAPTER 19

Leo sat on the floor of the Drift-a-long command module and groaned. He stared at the heap of junk in the other corner.

'Are we there yet?' the heap of junk asked.

The Drift-a-long bumped once more, then started to swing from side to side. Leo wailed this time. 'Not yet, Isaac. I'll tell you when we're near.'

Another bump, with an extra shudder, jolted Leo. The whole command module shook. 'I'm not even going to try to put myself together,' Isaac said. 'With so much shaking, I'll only fall apart again.'

Mina was standing tall and proud at the controls. She was the only one of them who had enjoyed the lurching, swaying and bounding of the Drift-a-long. 'Hold on! The beanbag has just stolen a speedboat!'

Leo closed his eyes. That lumpy red beanbag might have looked innocent, but over the last few hours they'd watched it steal a motorbike,

a skateboard, a ride-on lawnmower, a bus, a hovercraft and now a speedboat. It might be plush but it was cunning. The way it used its lumpiness to wrestle that bus driver out of her seat was the most amazing thing he'd seen since My Little Brainy had burped 'Happy Birthday' on Ragnar's birthday.

'Enough!' Ragnar yelled from inside a cupboard. 'I can't take anymore!'

'It's all right, Ragnar,' Leo managed to say. He swallowed, nearly losing it as the Drift-a-long suddenly swooped up and down. 'We'll be there soon.'

The cupboard door opened to reveal the pig lying on the bottom shelf and looking quite green. Leo wondered exactly what paints he'd need in order to create such a colour.

'It's not the Drift-a-long,' Ragnar moaned. 'I ate three cakes in a row.'

Before Leo could reprimand Ragnar for eating their entire supply of cakes, Mina whooped.

'We're heading for an island,' she called out. 'I think this might be it!'

CHAPTER 20

Carefully, Leo got to his feet and joined Mina at the controls. Isaac pulled himself together and clanked up alongside them. Ragnar sighed and squeezed out of the cupboard. He trotted over to the viewing window Leo had made especially for him.

'There's a mountain in the middle of the island,' Mina reported. 'It's surrounded by jungle. And on top of it is an enormous castle shaped like a lounge suite – two chairs and a couch – surrounded by a huge wall.'

'Hmm . . .' Leo rubbed his chin. 'I don't know.'

'And there's a big sign out the front: NOTHING TO SEE HERE. MOVE ALONG.'

'Ha!' Leo said as the motion of the Drift-a-long eased. 'Nice try, supervillain!'

Mina pointed down below. 'It must be the right place. Look at the beanbag.'

The beanbag had just beached the speed-boat on the island's shore. It lumped itself out and crawled onto the chairlift that ran up the side of the mountain to the lounge-suite-shaped castle.

'I like the chairs on that chairlift,' Isaac said. 'The stripy fabric is very decorative.'

Ragnar frowned. 'Are you saying that it's a Lounge Chair Lift?'

Leo shook his head. 'I'd say it's an Easychair Lift. This Furniture Overlord has impressive powers.'

The walls surrounding the castle were high, thick and impressive. A huge gate opened just as the beanbag got there and it scampered inside.

'Good enough,' Leo said. 'Let's check out the place first. Mina, can you circle around a few times?'

Ragnar grunted. 'Nice and easy circles, all right?'

Mina sent the Drift-a-long into a slow, calm loop. Leo used the binoculars. Though the place appeared deserted, he had his suspicions. He looked for furniture of any kind, but the courtyard was empty and the gatehouse was bare. There was nothing on top of the walls. 'You know,' he said, 'I think this entire castle is made of wood.'

'The Furniture Overlord must like the natural look,' Mina said.

'Clean and modern wooden furniture suits any home,' Leo added.

Mina looked at him. 'Huh?'

'I think I saw that in an advertisement,' Leo said quickly. 'But there's no time for that now. We're going in.'

'Good,' Mina said. 'This circling is making me dizzy.'

'Ragnar, time to get on deck,' Leo called. 'Isaac, are you ready?'

Isaac shook himself. Only a few nuts and bolts fell off. 'I feel tip-top,' he said. 'Perhaps I should go to pieces more often.'

'As long as you've got good buddies to help you get back together again,' Ragnar pointed out.

'Exactly.' Isaac flicked a tiny bit of rust off his shoulder. 'Perhaps everyone should do it. Would you like to try when we return to headquarters?'

Ragnar backed away. 'I'm much too complicated to be reassembled easily.'

'No time for that now,' Leo said. 'We have an evil supervillain to stop. Mina, can you bring us in close?'

'Sure can,' Mina said. 'There's a handy supervehicle parking lot right outside.'

'Is it free, or are there meters?' Leo asked.

Mina squinted. 'Looks like it's free.'

Leo swung the binoculars around. The concrete area next to the castle had rocky jungle on three sides. It was the only flat spot for kilometres. 'Take her down then, Mina.'

Leo went to the rear of the command module. He opened all three of the big metal lockers that stood against the wall.

'Isaac, Ragnar,' he called, 'time to get weaponed up.'

Ragnar whistled. Leo thought that was pretty clever for a pig. 'So many choices,' the pig said. 'Do I want a MoonBuster or an Evaporator? Could I strap on that Jelly Bean Booster as a backup? Ooh, I like the look of that one. Shiny! Is it new? What is it?'

'It's a vacuum cleaner. You're in the broom closet.' Leo closed the closet door. 'After the success you and Mina had with the duct tape last time, what about the Spaghetti Shooter?'

'Spaghetti Shooter?' Ragnar's curly tail quivered with excitement. 'Is it as cool as it sounds?'

'It's an old reliable,' Leo said. 'I used it to take down Mega Meg.'

Leo took the Spaghetti Shooter from the rack. It was good and solid, one of his best-ever weapons. It shot out epoxy-carbon-fibre-reinforced spaghetti – huge long lengths of it. It was bulkier than the SuperSilly String Cannon, but more effective against heavy foes.

'It shoots spaghetti?' Ragnar said. 'Not overcooked, I hope.'

Leo winced. 'Of course not. Super al dente.'

Isaac took up a large sack of Superglue Bombs.

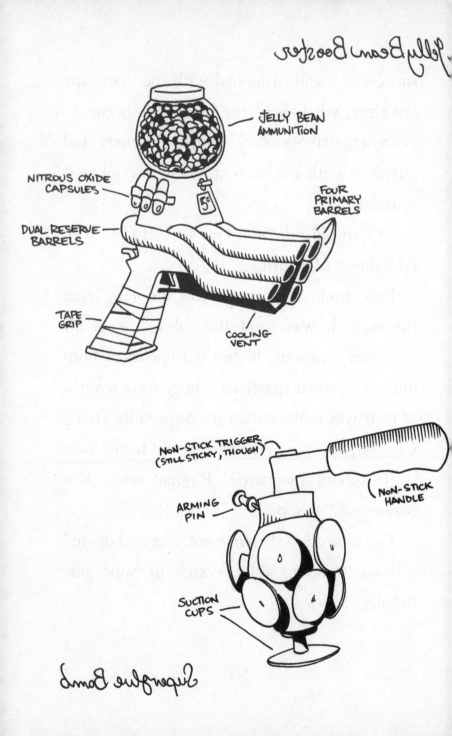

Jelly Bean Booster

JELLY BEAN
AMMUNITION

NITROUS OXIDE
CAPSULES

5¢

FOUR
PRIMARY
BARRELS

DUAL RESERVE
BARRELS

TAPE
GRIP

COOLING
VENT

NON-STICK TRIGGER
(STILL STICKY, THOUGH)

NON-STICK
HANDLE

ARMING
PIN

SUCTION
CUPS

Superglue Bomb

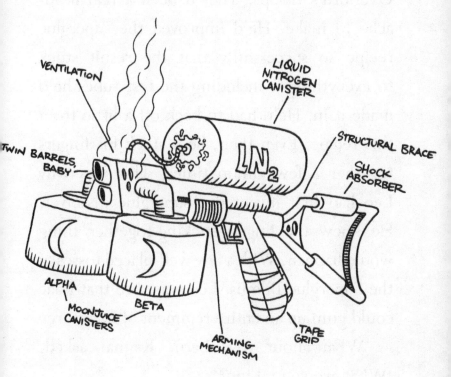

VENTILATION

LIQUID NITROGEN CANISTER

TWIN BARRELS, BABY

STRUCTURAL BRACE

SHOCK ABSORBER

LN₂

ALPHA

MOONJUICE CANISTERS

BETA

ARMING MECHANISM

TAPE GRIP

MoonEustor

Leo nodded his approval – they were the perfect thing for battling the Furniture Overlord's troops. They'd been a real headache to make. He'd improved the superglue recipe so successfully that the result stuck to everything – including the test tubes he'd made it in. He'd had to back off a little from this recipe. Even then, he'd stuck his fingers together a few zillion times. This was why Leo had first invented a superglue dissolver. He knew the fingers-sticking-together thing would happen. With a few well-placed tosses of the Superglue Bombs, Leo was sure that Isaac could gum up an entire regiment of furniture.

'What about you, Leo?' Ragnar asked. 'What are you taking?'

'I've given it a lot of thought,' Leo said, reaching into the cabinet. 'It's time for Leonardo da Vinci to cut loose.'

CHAPTER 21

The obvious way to go was power tools, which were the natural enemy of all furniture. In the right hands, a router, an electric planer or a circular saw would strike fear into any wooden object. Leo hadn't had time to work his magic on anything from the hardware shop, so he'd packed another old favourite — the really noisy Roarer Borer.

It had started life as a coffee grinder until Leo had had the bright idea to combine it with the insides of a tumble dryer for that extra bit of oomph. He'd stripped it down and powered it through a microneutronium reactor he'd whipped up in between studying the anatomy of horses (at the time he thought making a great big horse statue was just what the world needed).

At first, he'd imagined that the Roarer Borer would be useful for putting extra holes into wedges of Swiss cheese. It shot out dozens of whirling balls of force that burrowed through just about anything — furniture included.

Leo cradled the Roarer Borer in his arms.

The metal-and-plastic weapon fitted his shoulder perfectly. It felt good to have it, but just in case, he had his top-secret weapon with him.

He patted the small box hooked onto his belt. It was his last resort, his last-chance backup, the sort of thing he didn't want to use unless he had to. He hadn't had time to test it, either, so he hoped that if he had to use it, it'd work.

Sometimes it was tough being a super-genius inventor and world-saver. Everyone depended on you in a crisis, and Leo was starting to realise that he didn't want to let people down – especially his friends. Considering this, he added 'Not wanting to let them down' to his What Makes A Good Friend List.

Mina landed the Drift-a-long and turned to Leo. 'I want the Commander Sander.'

'Are you sure?' Leo asked. 'You have to get close to the enemy in order to use the Commander Sander and it leaves a lot of sawdust afterwards.'

Mina nodded seriously. 'That's just what I want. Give me two – one for each hand. I'll wipe the smiles off their faces.'

'I don't think furniture actually smiles,' Isaac said helpfully. 'Not unless it's covered in a nice smiley-face print, of course.'

'Well, they won't be smiling if they come up against me,' Mina said.

Leo thought about this for a moment. 'It sounds like you're angry, Mina.'

'Well noticed, Leo,' Mina said. 'Angry is what I am.'

'Any particular reason?' Leo asked. 'I mean, apart from someone wanting to take over the world.'

Mina sighed. 'It's not that,' she said. 'That happens all the time. What I don't like is the way he's using furniture to do it.'

'I know how you feel,' Ragnar said. 'Furniture has been with us forever and this wallpaper wally has turned it against us.'

Mina nodded. 'That's right. Good old furniture – it's everywhere, and they're using it. Our house is full of furniture, and if this supervillain gets going, that means my mum and dad won't be safe.'

Leo smacked his fist into his palm. 'So let's go and stop him. Everyone ready?'

They poured out of the command module.

Leo tried to look in all directions at once

as they ran up to the colossal gate. 'Keep an eye out,' he advised. 'Any furniture we find around here will probably be dazed as the outdoors isn't their normal habitat.'

Mina ran up to the gate. 'It's locked!' she cried.

'Stand back,' Leo ordered.

He used a moderate setting and pulled the trigger of the Roarer Borer. With a sound like a hundred angry chainsaws, a dozen balls of power leapt out and punched right through the black wood of the gate. Leo walked over and kicked it. A whole section of the gate and the wall next to it crumbled. Leo wiped the wood dust from his arm. 'At International Fixit Inc., we make our own entrances.'

'And the Furniture Overlord imprisons people who try to stop him,' a giant voice boomed. 'Especially those who bore holes through his gates. It's going to take me ages to mend that!'

From out of the jungle poured picnic benches, trestle tables, banana lounges, sun chairs and dozens of flapping patio umbrellas.

Leo groaned. He'd forgotten about outdoor furniture!

CHAPTER 22

More outdoor furniture burst out of the jungle and surrounded them. Even a giant, hulking hot tub came waddling and splashing over.

'Throw down your weapons!' The Furniture Overlord's voice echoed from the speakers high on the walls.

Leo saw movement out of the corner of his eye and turned, bringing up the Roarer Borer. But it was too late. Something dropped on him from above. In seconds he was tangled and lashed up so tightly he couldn't move. The same happened to Mina, Isaac and Ragnar. None of them even got off a shot.

Leo struggled until a wooden rod whacked him on the head and he saw stars.

The courtyard rang with the Furniture Overlord's laughter. 'Well done, Flying Hammock Squad! Now, drag them to the dungeons!'

CHAPTER 23

'You have to agree,' Ragnar said, 'this place is straight out of the dungeon textbook.'

Leo didn't answer. He was busy scratching out plans on the wall with a paperclip. He'd decided to go alphabetical this time and was up to Plan G – in between a few asides.

The paperclip was all that was left after they'd been stripped of their weapons. Even Leo's Usefulness Belt, along with his top-secret weapon, had been taken. The weapons had been secured in a locker next to the dungeon. Leo could read the CONFISCATED ENEMY WEAPONS sign through the bars of their cell door.

He'd had no idea that table lamps could use their cords like octopus tentacles. They were very clever that way. It gave him an idea for a bicycle that used tentacles instead of wheels. He began to fill up another wall with sketches, including one of a lady with a white ferret, because ferrets were cool. That's what Mina had told him, anyway.

'You're not getting distracted again, are you?' Mina said. 'You're supposed to be

getting us out of here, not doing more of your drawings.'

'Sorry,' Leo mumbled. He tilted his head. He wasn't sure he had the ferret's nose right but it could wait.

The door to their cell opened and a coffee table waddled in. Leo was about to make a run for it when he saw the shadow of a large sideboard standing guard just outside.

The coffee table had a speaker sitting on it.

'Follow the table,' came the Furniture Overlord's voice.

'What if we refuse?' Ragnar snapped.

'You'll be put in a kitchen dresser and dragged along.'

Ragnar's ears drooped. 'I was just asking. No need to get all snippy.'

The sideboard fell in behind them as

they left the cell. It was long, low, made of dark mahogany and had enough scratches and marks to show that it had been around. That was one tough piece of furniture, Leo thought.

The coffee table led them through a maze of corridors lined with furniture. Though none of it moved, Leo had the distinct feeling they were being watched. Watched *and* judged.

Two giant doors sprung to life and opened into a large hall. Furniture of all sorts moved aside, creating an aisle for them to pass through. Leo stopped and swallowed, only to have the sideboard nudge him forward.

He saw straw furniture, Japanese furniture, metal furniture, antique furniture, cheap furniture, office furniture, garden furniture, leather furniture and even blow-up furniture.

'Don't worry,' Mina whispered to him. 'We'll take care of these discount rejects soon enough.'

Leo managed a smile. Her brave words comforted him.

They marched alongside Isaac and Ragnar right down the middle of the hall and up to the Furniture Overlord.

CHAPTER 24

Standing on the stage was the Furniture Overlord himself. Behind him were two girls and a boy dressed in flunkey uniforms. They were snarling.

As they approached, Leo sized up their latest superenemy.

The Furniture Overlord had straight black hair and a broad grin and was wearing the most ridiculous supervillain costume Leo had ever seen – and that was saying something. After all, Leo had battled the Human Watering Can and kept a straight face. He'd caught Stapler Girl and not cracked up. He'd put the Iron Donut behind bars without laughing. In some ways, they had all been good practice for this very moment.

The Furniture Overlord had a wooden crown, which was reasonable. It had some nice cane inserts, at least. But that was the best part of the costume. On his feet were slippers made out of upholstery fabric – the kind with big cheesy flowers on it. His arms and legs were clothed in bright-green lycra. He was holding a small footstool in his arms and stroking it.

Between his neck and his knees was a chest of drawers. Now, if Leo were master of the world's furniture and had to have a super-villain costume, he might just have lycra-ed up and put a logo on his chest. Maybe a stylish wardrobe in gold, or a rocker recliner – something tasteful.

The Furniture Overlord, on the other hand, had gone way over the top. His costume had row upon row of drawers from neck to knee, back and front. Leo stared as the Furniture Overlord opened one, fumbled around in it and found a pen to scratch something on a document one of his human flunkeys had given him.

His human flunkeys were much better off. Although they were also decked out in lycra, they only had to wear furniture hats. One was in the shape a three-legged stool, one was a wastepaper basket and one was a magazine rack.

The Furniture Overlord stepped forward. With that stupid costume, he wasn't exactly Mr Speedy. 'Admit that you have been defeated! Bow down before the Furniture Overlord, the leader of the Furniture Army!'

'Okay, okay,' Leo said, bowing.

'What are you doing?' Mina whispered.

'Bowing to a goofy kid in a chest of drawers.'

'What?' Mina clenched her fists. 'Never!'

'Go on,' Leo said. 'It won't hurt and it doesn't mean anything. After all, who's to know?'

Mina's eyebrows shot up. 'Good point.'

The Furniture Overlord laughed. 'The robot and the pig, too.'

Isaac took his cue from Leo and Mina and clanked out a bow. All eyes turned to the pig.

Ragnar sniffed. 'You want a pig to bow? How?'

'No time for dog noises,' Leo said. 'Just drop onto your front knees.'

'Sheesh, the things I do,' Ragnar grumbled. He dropped. 'Ow! Hurties!'

'Excellent.' The Furniture Overlord rocked back on his heels and laughed. 'We've recorded that and it'll make a nice animated GIF to share everywhere!'

Mina shot Leo a look. 'Who's to know? The whole world, Leo, that's who.'

CHAPTER
25

Leo thought it a good time to slip in a question. 'So what's with this obsession with furniture?' he asked.

The Furniture Overlord frowned. 'Nothing, really,' he said with a shrug. 'I just wanted a way to conquer the world and no one had done furniture yet. And once you have a theme, you have to stick with it. It's in the supervillain handbook.'

Leo had heard of this supervillain handbook. He wondered if he could get hold of a copy for Wild Wilbur. 'I suppose you have to be consistent.'

'Exactly,' the Furniture Overlord said. 'Sometimes I wish I'd chosen something a bit more ferocious, like wild animals or sharks

or something. Furniture is a bit limiting, really.'

The assembled furniture milled about with embarrassment.

'That's no good,' Leo said sympathetically.

'And this costume gets really hot,' the Furniture Overlord went on, 'and itchy sometimes and . . . What am I saying? I AM THE FURNITURE OVERLORD! MWAHAHAHAHA! THROW THEM IN THE DUNGEON!'

The big doors at the rear of the hall swung open. A tea trolley trundled in and rattled up the aisle.

'What is this?' the Furniture Overlord barked. He crossed his arms and rested them on the top row of drawers. 'I won't be interrupted in my gloating.'

'He does a pretty good gloat,' Ragnar admitted. 'He's right up there with the best gloaters I've heard.'

The tea trolley barged right between Leo and Mina. It rolled up to the steps. Sitting on top of the trolley was a large rectangular box. A card was stuck on its lid.

The Furniture Overlord wobbled to the front of the stage. He bent over and studied the card. 'A delivery for International Fixit Inc.? In my top-secret hide-out lair citadel? Unthinkable!'

'Who's it from?' Leo asked.

'From some cheeky, ignorant, foolish clown who calls himself Wild Wilbur!' The Furniture Overlord was red in the face. 'Oh, wait, it's a box of chocolates.'

Leo stepped forward. 'Stop that. Those

chocolates are the property of Fixit International Inc.'

Ragnar groaned. Isaac put a metal hand to his metal forehead with a metal *clank*.

'Don't worry,' Leo whispered to them, out of the corner of his mouth. 'I know what I'm doing. Get ready to escape. We'll use Plan D.'

Isaac covered his face with his hands. 'Please, not Plan D.'

Ragnar chortled. 'Plan D. I was hoping we'd use Plan D.'

The Furniture Overlord straightened. His doors creaked. His drawers shook with anger. 'This is *my* top-secret lair hide-out citadel castle! I say who belongs to what – and those chocolates are now MINE.' He peered at the box. 'I hope there's peppermint cream. That's my favourite.'

Leo shook his fist. 'If there's one thing you could do to hurt Fixit International Inc., that would be to eat their chocolates.'

It was Mina's turn to groan. 'He'll never fall for that,' she muttered.

'Flunkeys!' roared the Furniture Overlord. 'Open this box immediately!'

'On the other hand,' Mina added, 'he could fall for it like a ton of bricks.'

Leo edged backwards. 'Get ready.'

The three flunkeys sprang to help their master. They wrestled and jostled. The trolley rocked a little. While the Furniture Overlord leaned forward, the flunkeys worked off the top of the box.

With a sad puff, the top layer of chocolates sprang upwards. The Furniture Overlord copped a faceful.

'OW! OW! OW! MY NOSE!' he screeched.
'THOSE ARE HARD CENTRES!'

'Let's go!' Leo shouted.

The last thing he saw was three frightened flunkeys and an assortment of lamps, trolleys and tables clustered around the Furniture Overlord. He was staggering around the stage, his drawers shooting open and crashing shut.

'I'M NOT HURT!' he roared, batting them away. 'I'M JUST VERY EMBARRASSED! STOP THEM!'

CHAPTER
26

At the Furniture Overlord's command,
all the furniture in the hall moved to block
International Fixit Inc.'s escape. But Plan D
was in full swing.

Isaac sighed and put his arms by his sides,
making himself rigid. Leo and Mina then

picked him up and laid him on top of Ragnar, facedown.

'Oof!' the pig grunted. 'Have you put on weight, Iron Belly? You need to keep an eye on your wood intake.'

'I assure you that I am the perfect weight for a robot of my height and construction,' Isaac retorted.

'No time for that now.' Leo grabbed one

of Isaac's arms. Mina stood on the other side and grabbed the other. 'It's time for ramming speed!'

With a grunt, Ragnar started off. With Leo and Mina's assistance, the pig soon had a good trot going.

A bookcase stumbled in front of them but was swiftly smashed aside.

'Whee!' Ragnar squealed, breaking into a

gallop. 'That's the way, Tinny! That's using your –'

'Don't,' Isaac said. 'Just don't.'

Leo and Mina guided the way. They crashed through a pair of bar stools and battered an antique roll-top desk, which then fell back and crushed a pair of table lamps.

The whole hall was in uproar.

'Stop them!' bellowed the Furniture Overlord. 'I COMMAND YOU TO STOP THEM!'

The wave of terrified furniture spread outwards. Wall cupboards toppled on glass tables, shattering them into a thousand tiny pieces. Entertainment units fell on bedside tables. Futons were flung metres away and tangled with banana lounges.

'Where's the Flying Hammock Squad?'

the Furniture Overlord howled. 'SEND IN THE HAMMOCKS!'

But it was too late. Fixit International Inc. was already through the doors and hurtling into the castle.

CHAPTER 27

'Which way is out?' Mina panted.

'Not out,' Leo said. 'We have to find our weapons.'

'To the dungeons, then,' Ragnar said. 'But first, get this copper-bottomed bozo off me.'

Isaac moaned as Leo and Mina helped him

to his feet. 'Oh, my aching head,' he said. 'I need a can of oil and a good lie-down.'

'No time for that now,' Leo reminded them. The sound of pursuing furniture echoed down the hall. 'This way!'

Mina and Leo helped Isaac down the stairs and along the corridor to the dungeons. The robot clutched his head all the way. They stopped at the Confiscated Enemy Weapons locker, complete with massive padlock. Standing in their way was a brutal-looking couch.

It was a bruiser. Its brown vinyl hide was torn and patched. The back rest looked as if it had been slashed with heavy weapons. On its middle cushion was a bunch of keys.

Leo whirled around. Their pursuers could be heard charging down the stairs.

Mina touched his arm. 'Leave it to me.' She hopped on one foot and took off a shoe. Then she hopped on her socked foot and whipped off the other. 'Won't be a second.'

'Wait,' Leo said. 'Be careful.'

'Aren't I always?' Mina grinned before skating off across the polished floorboards.

Leo stared. Mina was going much faster than walking, much faster than running. Her hair stretched back in the wind as she bent down low.

The couch didn't move as Mina zoomed closer. Just before Mina reached it, she flexed her knees and jumped. She soared right over the couch, reaching down as she flew and snatching the keys. She landed neatly, somersaulted to the Confiscated Enemy Weapons locker and opened it.

The couch heaved itself around and reared up on its hind legs. It was about to launch at Mina when it noticed the Commander Sanders in her hands.

'Time to do a bit of dusting,' she said, and rammed the weapons home.

With a sound like a concrete mixer inside a tumble dryer while the world's biggest pencil sharpener went to work, Mina disappeared behind a cloud of sawdust and shredded vinyl.

A few seconds later, she was standing in front of a waist-high pile of pulverised wood and plastic. 'What are you waiting for?' she said to Leo. 'Throw me my shoes and let's get this job done!'

'Excellent work!' Leo said as he hurried towards her. 'We're on our way now!'

Mina grinned. 'I'd say that it's sofa so good.'

CHAPTER 28

The first thing Leo grabbed when he got to the locker was his Usefulness Belt. He checked if everything was there and sagged with relief.

A clatter and a shuffle from the stairs announced that their pursuers had arrived.

The Furniture Overlord stood at the head of a horde of jostling, snarling furniture. 'Aha!' he cried. 'There is no escape! Why don't you turn around and stroll back into your cell?'

'Stop shouting,' Ragnar huffed. 'Isaac's got a headache.'

The Furniture Overlord put his hands on his top drawers and laughed.

'That's close enough,' Mina snapped. 'We're jam-packed with Leo's weapons. You'd better surrender.'

'I don't think so,' the Furniture Overlord said. 'You might be able to destroy some of my furniture army but you won't win. I have a manufacturing plant in the basement that is using my special processes to create millions of loyal furniture commandos!'

'Really?' Leo said, perking up. 'Sounds fascinating. I'd like to see that.'

Mina nudged him.

'Oh, right. Sorry.' He stood up straight. 'We aim to stop your evil plans, Furniture Overlord.' Leo plucked his top-secret weapon from his Usefulness Belt. He tapped it with a finger. 'And we have the means to do it.'

'Oooh, I'm so scared,' the Furniture Overlord said. 'What are you going to do? Turn me into a toothpick?'

'Not exactly. What I have in here are super-intelligent super-hungry super-termites. I release them, and your furniture army, your castle and your supervillain suit are history.'

The Furniture Overlord stared, then rocked back and laughed long and loud.

Mina frowned. 'Leo, is this something you whipped up just in case?'

'It was my backup backup plan, only to be used in emergencies,' Leo replied.

'Why?' Ragnar said. 'It sounds like the perfect plan to beat these guys.'

'I was rushed,' Leo said, 'and genetic engineering is tricky, you know. The thing is, there's a slight possibility that when these beasties finish their job here, they'll disobey my orders and keep on going. They could eat every wooden thing in the world.'

'What?' Ragnar squeaked. 'Even ping-pong bats?'

'Even ping-pong bats,' Leo said gravely.

'I think it's a risk we'll have to take,' Mina said. 'We trust you, Leo. I don't think you'd mess up like that.'

'Thank you,' Leo said. And there was the friend thing again. His dad was right. He added 'Friends trust each other' to his list.

'Seize them!' the Furniture Overlord bellowed.

Leo opened the box.

CHAPTER 29

The Furniture Overlord blinked in the strong sunlight. He was wearing nothing but his underwear. 'Where did my castle go?' he whimpered.

Leo let out a long sigh of relief. The super-intelligent super-hungry super-termites had zoomed back into their box when they were finished. He closed the lid, hooked the box onto his belt and folded his arms across his chest. 'Your evil schemes have come to nothing, Furniture Overlord. You face a long stretch in supervillain prison.'

The Furniture Overlord's shoulders slumped and his face fell. 'Cho.'

'What?'

'Cho – that's my name. Look around. I'm not the Furniture Overlord anymore. I'm just plain Cho.'

'Well, Just Plain Cho,' Leo said, 'you'll have to come with us.'

'Wait.' Cho held up a hand. 'What's the time?'

'It's nearly four-thirty,' Isaac said.

Cho frowned. 'What day is it again?'

'Sunday,' Mina replied.

'Look,' Cho said, spreading his hands, 'I've got school tomorrow.'

'Don't we all?' Mina said. 'Weekends go so fast, right?'

'That's what I mean,' Cho agreed. 'I haven't done my homework yet.'

'Oh, I see.' Leo rubbed his forehead. 'Look, supervillain prison is pretty good like that. We'll get you there quick as we can and they'll help you finish your homework.'

'Will they let me out to go to school tomorrow?' Cho asked.

'Yep,' Leo said with an encouraging smile. 'Under supervision, of course.'

Cho nodded. 'And they lock me up again after school?'

'That's the system,' Leo said.

Cho grinned. 'Excellent! Then I can do my homework with no distractions. This conquering-the-world business makes school really hard, you know.'

CHAPTER
30

After dropping the ex-Furniture Overlord at the supervillain prison, International Fixit Inc. swapped the Drift-a-long for the Boomer Zoomer, a high-speed vehicle Leo kept at the prison for emergencies. They stormed back to Fixit International Inc. headquarters.

Leo stood with his hands on his hips and studied the Whiter-Than-Whiteboard. 'Right. The Furniture Overlord can be scratched from the To-do List, thanks to our efforts.'

'A fine job, indeed,' Isaac said. He clanked over, took up a duster and with one swipe erased the wannabe furniture ruler.

'That means Wild Wilbur moves up a spot,' Ragnar said, trotting into the room. He looked around uneasily. 'Hey, did anyone check for explosive food when we came in?'

'I did,' Mina said. 'All I found was that birthday cake.'

Everyone turned towards the chocolate cake sitting on the bench. It was big, round and had lots of suspicious candles. They blinked at each other.

'Is it actually someone's birthday today?' Leo asked.

'Look,' Ragnar said, 'I don't like to point this out since it does seem like a cake and all, but it could be dangerous.'

Leo peered at the cake. The white piping on the chocolate icing read: *4 Internationale Fixit Inc.* ☺ *WW*

'Those candles could be dynamite,' Isaac said.

Mina shook her head. 'Nope, I got rid of the TNT candles.'

'You've made it harmless?' Leo said. 'Good work!'

Mina shrugged. 'This is Fixit International, so I fixed it.'

A thump shook the door. Ragnar squealed. Isaac jumped back and a handful of nuts and bolts fell from his joints. Mina's hand went straight to her belt and grabbed a roll of duct tape.

Leo's eyes narrowed. 'Who is it?' he called out. The door shook again, but this time the thump was less mighty. 'Stand back,' Leo whispered to his friends.

'It's Wild Wilbur, I know it,' Ragnar said hoarsely. 'Let me get my Lamington Accelerator.'

Leo held up a hand to stay the pig. He reached out, grabbed the doorhandle and flung the door open. A tattered, dirty and smelly red velvet beanbag fell through the doorway. It was covered in leaves and rubbish.

'Lumpy!' Ragnar cried. 'He must have survived the destruction of the Furniture Overlord's lair of evil solitude!'

'He crawled all this way back to us,' Mina said. 'Unbelievable.'

Leo crouched down to inspect the grubby fabric. 'From the oil stains and the airline boarding passes, I don't think he crawled *all* the way.'

Mina stood on her tiptoes and looked out of the window. 'There's a hot air balloon out in the yard. I think Lumpy is even more cunning than we thought.'

'Can we keep him?' Ragnar pleaded, jumping up and down. 'He followed us home, so can we keep him? Pretty please?'

Leo nodded. 'He's your new friend, is he?'

'Yeah!' Ragnar said. He thrust his snout close to the ragged survivor. 'You're a *good* beanbag. Aren't you, Lumpy? Attaboy!'

Leo watched closely. 'And why exactly is

he your friend? What do you like about him? What does he like about you?'

Mina tapped him on the shoulder. 'Relax, Leo. They're friends – that's all. It happens.'

Leo scratched his chin. 'But I want to know all about friends so I can be a good one. I'm making a list, you see.'

'Another list?' Mina grinned at him and gave him a light punch on the shoulder. 'Leo, you don't need a list for friending. You already know how to be a great friend.'

Leo's eyebrows shot up. 'I do?'

'You bet,' Mina said. 'Now, let's see what's next on our To-do List. How's that undersea monster off the coast of Chile going?'

MICHAEL PRYOR has published more than thirty fantasy books and over forty short stories, from literary fiction to science fiction to slapstick humour. Michael has been shortlisted six times for the Aurealis Awards, has been nominated for a Ditmar award, and six of his books have been Children's Book Council of Australia Notable Books. Michael's most recent books include The Chronicles of Krangor series for young readers, The Laws of Magic series and The Extraordinaires series for older readers, as well as *10 Futures*, a collection of interlinked stories imagining what our next 100 years might be like, and middle-grade technothriller *Machine Wars*. For more information about Michael and his books, visit www.michaelpryor.com.au.

JULES FABER is a multi-award-winning cartoonist and illustrator. He has published numerous comic strips, worked for various newspapers, taught cartooning around Australia, been in multiple art exhibitions and has worked as an animator on a Disney show. And on top of all that, he loves illustrating children's books, including Anh Do's WeirDo series (Scholastic), *Helix and the Arrival* by Damean Posner and the Leo da Vinci series by Michael Pryor.

HELP!

THE ICE-CREAM DOMINATION LEAGUE IS BLOWING UP THE WORLD'S ICE-CREAM FACTORIES!

ENTER LEO DA VINCI.

Inventor, artist, genius and founder of Fixit International Inc., all at the age of ten.

HIS TEAM?

Meet steam-powered Isaac, maths whiz and wise-cracking pig Ragnar, and Mina from school, who's super-handy with a hammer.

THE PLAN?

Ready the Strikebird. Pack the Heat-seeking Cauliflower Missiles. Find out why Comet Big-Kahuna is heading for Earth. Stop the IDL before Mum calls you home for dinner.

START THE CHEESY LAUNCH MUSIC AND HOLD ON FOR YOUR LIFE.

Available now!